MY BIBLE ALPHABET

By Maida Silverman

Illustrated by Kathy Mitchell

A GOLDEN BOOK • NEW YORK

Western Publishing Company, Inc., Racine, Wisconsin 53404

A ARK

Come into the ark, thou, and thy sons, and thy wife, and thy sons' wives with thee. And of every living thing...two of every sort shalt thou bring into the ark...

Genesis 6:18-19

The Lord told a good man named Noah to build a great boat, or ark. Noah built the ark of cypress wood. He filled the cracks with reeds. He spread tar over the reeds to make the ark waterproof.

The ark floated on the waters when the Lord sent a flood to cover the earth.

B BREAD

Bread was the most important food that people ate in Bible times. It was made fresh every day.

Grain was ground into flour. Flour was mixed with water and salt to make dough. The dough was rolled into round, flat cakes called loaves and baked on hot stones.

C CAMEL

And the Queen of Sheba came to Jerusalem with...camels that bore spices, and very much gold, and precious jewels...

I Kings 10:2

The people of the Bible used camels to carry heavy loads. Camels can travel many days without food or water. They can walk on soft, hot desert sands without sinking in.

D DESERT

And they thirsted not when He led them through the desert: He caused the water to flow out of the rocks for them…

Isaiah 48:21

The desert is a dry wilderness of sand and rocks. After Moses led the people of Israel out of Egypt, they wandered forty years in the desert.

E EGYPT

And Israel dwelt in the land of Egypt…

Genesis 47:27

Egypt is an ancient land. The people of Israel lived in Egypt for many years before Moses led them away to the Promised Land.

F FISH

The people of the Bible liked to catch and eat fish.
Fishermen fished from the shore and from boats. The
fish they caught were carried to market in baskets.

Jesus' disciples Andrew, James, John, Nathanael, and
Peter were fishermen. They often went fishing together.

G GAMES

Children in Bible times loved to play games. Girls liked juggling and playing catch. Boys enjoyed playing tug-of-war. Everyone liked to spin tops and roll hoops. Babies played with toy animals that had wheels for feet.

H HONEY

Jonathan...stretched out...his hand and dipped it in a honeycomb, and put his hand to his mouth, and his countenance brightened....

I Samuel 14:27

Honey was a favorite food in Bible times. Everyone liked to eat it. It was often given as a gift.

I IVORY

King Solomon made a great throne of ivory, and overlaid it with the finest gold....

I Kings 10:18

Ivory comes from the tusks of elephants. In Bible times, ivory was used to make furniture, boxes, and jewelry. Ivory was often decorated with gold and precious jewels.

J

JERUSALEM

If I forget thee, O Jerusalem, let my right hand wither!...if I do not exalt Jerusalem above my chief joy....

Psalm 137:5-6

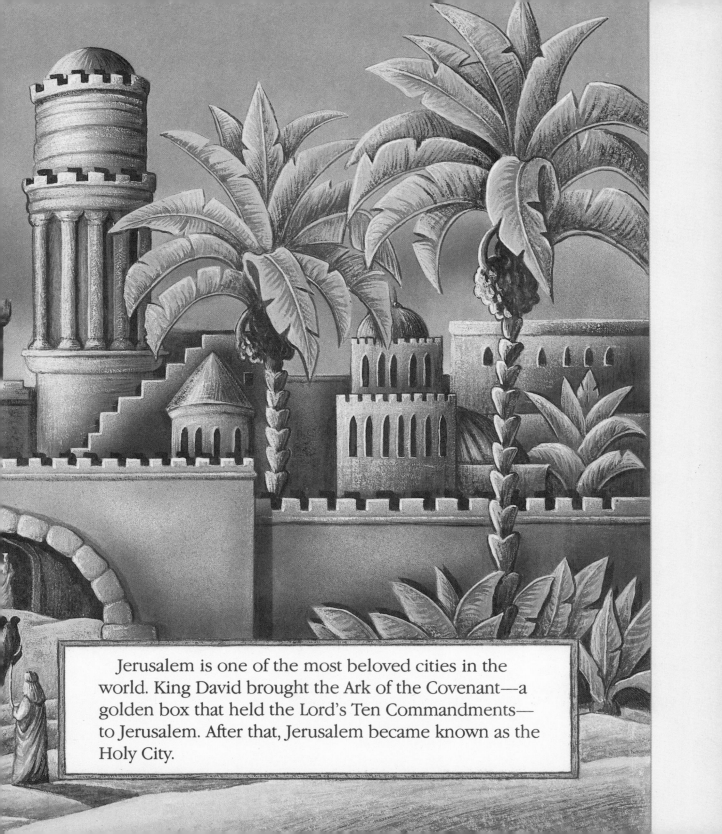

Jerusalem is one of the most beloved cities in the world. King David brought the Ark of the Covenant—a golden box that held the Lord's Ten Commandments—to Jerusalem. After that, Jerusalem became known as the Holy City.

K KID

*Feed thy kids beside the shepherds'
tents....*

The Song of Solomon 1:8

A kid is a baby goat. Abraham, Isaac, and Jacob had
large flocks of goats and kids. Children took care of the
kids. Kids were gentle and made good pets.

L LION

*A lion...is the mightiest among
beasts...*

Proverbs 30:30

Lions were very common in Bible times. They lived
in the mountains and deserts. People admired their
strength and feared them.

M MUSIC

The people of the Bible enjoyed music. David was a shepherd boy who was also a fine musician. He played the harp for King Saul.

N NILE

She took...a basket...put the child in it and placed it among the reeds at the river's bank....

Exodus 2:3

The Nile is a great river that flows through the land of Egypt. Crocodiles and many kinds of fish swim in the Nile. In Bible times, hippopotamuses lived along its shores.

When Moses was a baby, his mother hid him among the reeds that grew in the Nile. She saved him from being killed by the cruel king of Egypt.

OLIVE

The trees...said unto the olive tree,
"Reign thou over us!"...

Judges 9:8

The people of Israel called the olive the King of Trees. They prized its fruit and fine oil.

P PALM

A great crowd...took branches of
palm trees and went out to meet
him, crying, "Hosannah!"...

John 12:12-13

Palm trees were symbols of joy for people in Bible times. People enjoyed dates, the sweet fruit of the date palm tree.

Q QUAIL

The quails came up and covered the camp...

Exodus 16:13

Quail are small birds. In Bible times, they flew in huge flocks over great distances. The wind carried them over the desert.

Quail nourished the people of Israel while they wandered in the desert.

R RAISIN

Abigail...took...a hundred clusters of raisins...and laid them on donkeys....

I Samuel 25:18

Raisins are dried sweet grapes. They were a favorite food in Bible times. Children sometimes prepared raisins. They laid clusters of red, purple, and white grapes in the hot sun to dry.

S SCHOOL

In early Bible times, children were taught by their parents. They learned about crafts and farming.

In Jesus' time, children went to school and had a teacher. They were taught reading, writing, and arithmetic. Boys had to start going to school when they were six years old. Girls did not have to go unless they wanted to.

T TABLE

So she sat beside the reapers, and he passed...grain to her, and she ate...

Ruth 2:14

During early Bible times, the table was a mat laid on the floor. It was made of woven or braided straw.

U UNICORN

God...hath...the strength of a unicorn....

Numbers 23:22

Unicorn means "one horn." The unicorn of the Bible was a wild ox. It really had two horns. But pictures of the wild ox showed it from one side, and the two horns looked like one. So people called the wild ox a unicorn.

V VINEYARD

A certain man planted a vineyard, and set a hedge about it, and digged a place for the wine vat, and built a tower....

Mark 12:1

Grapevines were planted in vineyards. The first vineyard was planted by Noah after the flood.

W WELL

And he made the camels to kneel down...by the well of water at the time...that women go out to draw water....

Genesis 24:11

A well is a deep shaft dug far into the earth. Water seeps into the well underground. The people of Israel lived in a land that was very dry and hot. Wells were as precious to them as gold.

X XERXES

So Esther was taken unto King Ahasuerus, into his house royal…

Esther 2:16

Xerxes was a king of Persia. In the Bible, he is called Ahasuerus.

The king took Esther, an Israelite maiden, into his palace. He came to love her greatly, and he made her his queen.

Y YOKE

I have bought five yoke of oxen…

Luke 14:19

A yoke is a frame made of wood and rope. It joins two animals together. In Bible times, a pair of oxen was yoked together to plow the earth before seed was planted.